# Encyclopedia Brown and the Case of the Sleeping Dog

## Read the other Encyclopedia Brown Books by Donald J. Sobol

# Encyclopedia Brown and the Case of the Sleeping Dog

DONALD J. SOBOL

Illustrated by Warren Chang

Delacorte Press

Published by
Delacorte Press
Bantam Doubleday Dell Publishing Group, Inc.
1540 Broadway
New York, New York 10036

**Library of Congress Cataloging-in-Publication Data**
Sobol, Donald J.
    Encyclopedia Brown and the case of the sleeping dog / Donald J. Sobol ; illustrated by Warren Chang.
        p.    cm.
    Summary: America's Sherlock Holmes in sneakers continues his war on crime in ten more cases, the solutions to which are found in the back of the book.
    ISBN 0-385-32576-2
    [1. Mystery and detective stories.]   I. Chang, Warren, ill.   II. Title.
PZ7.S68524Epaf   1998
[Fic]—dc21                                                                      97-34952
                                                                                  CIP
                                                                                  AC

Manufactured in the United States of America
September 1998
10 9 8 7 6 5 4 3 2 1
BVG

# Contents

**For my granddaughter,
Lauren Anne Sobol**

# The Case of the Shower Singers

**O**n the outside, Idaville looked like an ordinary seaside town. It had playgrounds, banks, and beautiful white beaches. It had churches, a synagogue, and two delicatessens.

On the inside, however, Idaville was unlike any other town. No one, grown-up or child, got away with breaking the law!

From coast to coast, police officers wondered. How did Idaville do it? *What was the secret?*

The Idaville police station stood on Harding Street. But the real headquarters for the war on crime was a red brick house at 13 Rover Avenue.

Here lived Mr. and Mrs. Brown and their only child, ten-year-old Encyclopedia, America's crime-buster in sneakers.

Mr. Brown was chief of police. He was brave and honest, and he was smart. Whenever he came up against a case he could not solve, he knew what to do.

He put on his hat and went home.

Encyclopedia solved the case at the dinner table. Usually he needed to ask but one question.

Mr. Brown would have liked to tell the world about his son. But who would take him seriously?

Who would believe that a fifth-grader might be the best detective on earth?

So Chief Brown kept Encyclopedia's crime-busting a family secret.

Encyclopedia never let slip a word about the help he gave his father. It would have sounded like boasting.

But there was nothing he could do about his nickname.

Only his parents and teachers called him by his given name, Leroy. Everyone else called him Encyclopedia.

An encyclopedia is a book or set of books filled with facts from A to Z. Encyclopedia had read more books than anyone, and he never forgot a thing. His pals said that when he thought hard, you could hear pages turning.

After saying grace Tuesday evening, Chief Brown sat silently at the dinner table, fussing with his vegetable soup.

Encyclopedia and his mother knew the signs. A case had Chief Brown puzzled. They waited for him to speak.

At last Chief Brown put down his spoon.

"You remember the state shower singing finals last week in the old Ritz movie theater?" he asked.

Encyclopedia and his mother had been there. The six

finalists had sung in a bathroom built on the stage. A rubber ducky had hung from the shower curtain.

"In the shower you let your guard down and just belt it out," Mrs. Brown said. "I liked Oscar March, the fireman, best."

"The winner will compete for the national title in a sing-off against the other state winners," Chief Brown said. "The national champion gets a big trophy from a soap company."

"And perhaps a call from a talent scout," Mrs. Brown added. "What is the problem, dear?"

"The state winner is supposed to be announced tomorrow at the Founder's Day celebration," Chief Brown said. "But we don't know who won."

He explained. The judging committee for the contest had voted by secret ballot. The chairwoman, Mrs. Galan, had counted the votes.

"Only Mrs. Galan knew the winner," said Chief Brown.

"Why all the hush-hush?" Mrs. Brown asked.

"Last year, one of the judges leaked the winner to the newspapers," Chief Brown said. "The story ran a day early. It took all the steam out of the awards program."

"If Mrs. Galan knows the winner, why worry?" Mrs. Brown asked.

"Because," Chief Brown replied, "she flew to Los Angeles three days ago. She expected to return tonight. But an earthquake hit there this morning. The airport is closed. The telephone lines are down. She can't be reached."

Encyclopedia listened in silence. He knew his mother

and father were going over the case for his sake. They wanted him to have all the facts.

"Mrs. Galan did leave a clue," Chief Brown said. "She gave the committee's secretary, Drew Smith, a sealed envelope with a code inside. It names the winner. Mrs. Galan said that if she wasn't back by three o'clock today and she couldn't get to a phone, Mr. Smith was to open the envelope and find someone to break the code."

"I don't understand how you came into the case," said Mrs. Brown.

"Drew Smith thinks I'm the one who has broken codes in the past," Chief Brown said, smiling at Encyclopedia. "He trusts me not to tell the winner's name to anyone but him."

"I hope Drew Smith gave you a copy of the code," Mrs. Brown said. "Leroy hasn't failed you yet."

Chief Brown took a sheet of paper from his breast pocket. He handed it to Mrs. Brown.

She read: "aria alter liver scar ale tan."

"All are common words except 'aria,' which means a tune or a solo performance," said Mrs. Brown, who had taught high-school English and other subjects.

She passed the sheet to Encyclopedia.

Chief Brown said, "If it's of any help, the names of the singers are Dale Manning, Walter Blake, Stan Z. Zamora, Oscar March, Maria Woods, and Oliver Grossman."

"Six singers," said Mrs. Brown. "What has—"

She stopped. Encyclopedia had closed his eyes. He always closed his eyes when he did his hardest thinking.

He thought really hard for a full minute. Then he opened his eyes.

He asked his one question.

"Does the chairwoman of the judging committee, Mrs. Galan, have a special interest in names, Dad?"

Chief Brown was not surprised by the question. Encyclopedia's one mystery-busting question usually was itself a mystery.

Chief Brown answered, "Mrs. Galan is writing a book called *Naming Your Baby*. It will have thousands of names for boys and girls."

"I might have guessed," Encyclopedia said.

"Leroy!" exclaimed Mrs. Brown. "Who won?"

"Yes, who?" Chief Brown asked.

"The winner," Encyclopedia said, "is—"

# Who is the winner?

### (Turn to page 61 for the solution to The Case of the Shower Singers.)

# The Case of the Invisible Writing

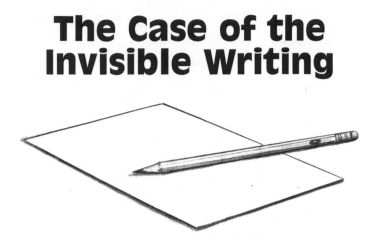

**E**ncyclopedia helped his father solve mysteries throughout the year. During the summer, he helped the children of the neighborhood as well.

When school let out, he opened his own detective agency in the garage. Every morning he hung out his sign:

## Brown Detective Agency
### 13 Rover Avenue
### LEROY BROWN
### President
No case too small
25¢ a day plus expenses

The first customer Thursday was Kitty Depugh.

She laid twenty-five cents on the gas can beside Encyclopedia.

"I want to hire you," she said. "Get back my grandma's pie before Bugs Meany eats it."

Bugs Meany was the leader of a gang of tough older boys. They called themselves the Tigers. They should have called themselves the Gift Factory. They were always giving some little kid the works.

"Suppose you tell me what happened," Encyclopedia said.

"Every Thursday I take one of Mom's homemade key lime pies to my grandma," Kitty began. "I was taking one to her half an hour ago."

"Bugs was watching for you?" Encyclopedia asked.

"He stopped me a block from Grandma's house," Kitty replied. "He offered to trade a magic flashlight that makes writing invisible for the pie."

"You believed him?" Encyclopedia asked.

"I had to have a look," Kitty admitted. "Bugs took me to his clubhouse and gave me a red pencil and a sheet of paper. He had me write my name. Then we went inside. He shut the door and suddenly it was pitch dark. I couldn't see a thing. I was scared."

"What then?" Encyclopedia inquired.

"Nothing. Bugs said the magic flashlight was broken. I'd have to come back when he had fixed it. He pushed me out of the clubhouse and kept the pie!"

"Our first step is to go see Bugs," Encyclopedia said.

Kitty shook her head. "No, thank you. A person can get hurt near Bugs."

"You've got to come," Encyclopedia insisted. "If you don't, how will I know the pie Bugs has is yours? Don't be afraid. I've handled Bugs before."

Kitty brightened a little. "Well, all right. But if anything happens, please notify my next of kin."

The Tigers' clubhouse was an unused, windowless toolshed behind Mr. Sweeney's auto body shop. Bugs was alone when Encyclopedia and Kitty arrived.

A pie in a green-and-brown dish rested on an empty orange crate by the door.

"That's my pie," Kitty said with relief. "Thank goodness Bugs hasn't eaten it yet."

At the sight of Encyclopedia, Bugs's face twisted into a sneer. "Well, well, look what crawled out of the Dumpster!"

Encyclopedia was used to Bugs's greetings. "Kitty claims you stole her key lime pie," he said calmly. "She was taking it to her grandmother."

"Little Red Riding Hood here has a shortage of brain cells," Bugs snarled. "No kid in her right mind dares call Bugs Meany a thief."

He threw back his head and roared, "I am overcome by unspeakable fury!"

Kitty retreated a step. "I just remembered," she whispered. "I don't want to be here."

Encyclopedia held her firmly by the arm.

"Kitty claims you were going to trade her a magic flashlight for the pie," he said to Bugs.

"The key lime pie you see before you I baked myself," Bugs retorted. "I am a master baker and a master at making things disappear."

"Come off it, Bugs," Encyclopedia said.

"Once I went too far, I confess it," Bugs said. "I made a pack mule invisible. The only way I could find him was by the smell of hay on his breath."

"Cut the comedy and let's see some writing disappear," Kitty challenged.

Bugs grinned. He led them into the clubhouse and handed Kitty the sheet of paper on which she'd signed her name.

He laid the sheet on an old stool. He took two flashlights from a shelf and shut the door.

It became black as coal inside the toolshed.

He shined a flashlight with a red bulb on the sheet.

Kitty gasped. "I don't see my name anymore!"

Bugs turned off the flashlight and turned on the other one. Under its white light, Kitty's name appeared clearly.

"You switched papers in the dark!" Kitty blurted out.

"No way," Bugs said. "I used a bulb rubbed red with a ruby from Baghdad, city of mystery. It makes writing disappear! To make the writing appear again, I used a bulb rubbed white with a sacred altar stone from ancient Egypt."

"Baloney," said Kitty.

"That does it!" Bugs bellowed. "Forget the trade! I'm keeping the pie *and* the magic flashlights. Now scram before I bend you out of shape!"

10

"I don't care to end up looking into my own ear," Kitty muttered to Encyclopedia. "Let's scram."

"Not without your key lime pie," Encyclopedia replied.

## How did Bugs make the writing disappear?

### (Turn to page 62 for the solution to The Case of the Invisible Writing.)

# The Case of the Stolen Fan

**B**ugs Meany hated being outsmarted by Encyclopedia all the time. He longed to get even.

The Tigers' leader dreamed of pressing the detective's belly button until his ears rang. But Bugs never used muscle. Whenever he felt like it, he remembered Sally Kimball.

Sally was Encyclopedia's junior partner in the Brown Detective Agency. She was also the prettiest girl in the fifth grade and the best athlete.

What's more, she had done what no little kid had thought possible. She had punched out big, bad Bugs.

The first time they had fought, Bugs had gone into his famous fighting stance. "This won't take long," he had boasted.

It hadn't.

Sally had walloped him—once.

Bugs had spun around and sat down. His eyes had glazed over, and his eyelids had started fluttering like moth wings.

"Remind me to get in touch with my lawyer," he'd moaned.

Sitting in the detective agency, Encyclopedia told Sally, "Bugs doesn't exactly love me, and you've driven him crazy. He thought he owned the neighborhood till you flattened him a few times. He won't rest until he gets even."

"Bugs is too dumb to get even," Sally snapped. "Ask his Aunt Eve. He still can't spell her name backwards."

"Don't sell him short," Encyclopedia warned quietly.

A sudden squeal of tires and a slam of metal nearby tore the air.

Sally jumped to her feet. "What an awful sound! Someone may be hurt."

The detectives ran to the scene. Two cars had banged fenders on Dunbary Street. People were still streaming from their homes and offices to see what had happened.

Encyclopedia caught sight of Bugs Meany. Bugs was standing in front of a house that doubled as a real estate office.

No one in either car was hurt. The drivers shouted at each other until the police arrived.

The police took charge. After twenty minutes, Encyclopedia and Sally returned to the detective agency.

"Uh-oh," Sally said. "We left the garage door open."

"There they are, the rotten little thieves!"

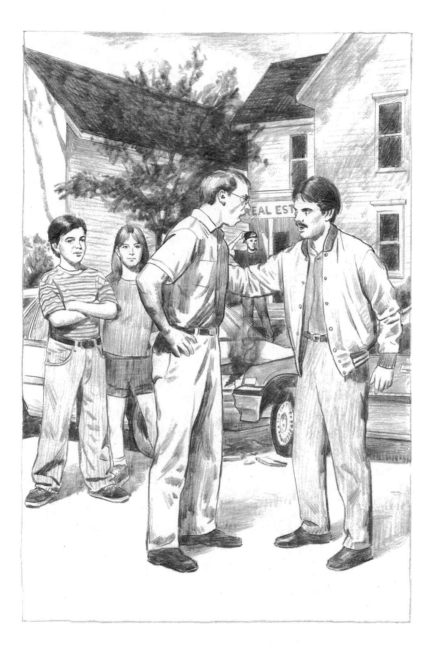

Bugs Meany came bounding out of the garage. Behind him was Officer Feldman.

"You'll learn crime doesn't pay!" Bugs jeered.

"Bugs claims you two stole a white electric fan from the desk of John Mann," Officer Feldman said.

"Who is John Mann?" Sally asked.

"He has a real estate office near where the accident happened," Officer Feldman said.

"I was walking past his office just before the accident," Bugs put in. "I saw Mr. Mann at his desk. He took a paper from his pocket and laid it in front of him. His desk fan blew the paper onto the floor."

"Did you see what was on the paper?" Officer Feldman asked.

"Naw, he'd just picked it up when the two cars hit each other," Bugs said. "He shoved the paper into his pocket and raced out to the accident."

"What did you see next?" Officer Feldman said.

"I saw these two goody-goods sneak into Mr. Mann's office," Bugs answered. "I didn't worry about them. I worried that someone in the accident might need my help."

"How did you know the fan was missing, Bugs?" Encyclopedia asked.

"I saw Mr. Mann come back to the office," Bugs replied. "I heard him yell, 'Someone stole my fan!' I figured it must be you two. I'm always thinking overtime."

"We never stole anything in our lives!" Sally protested.

Officer Feldman reached behind a sheet of plywood. He pulled out a small white fan.

"Bugs says he found the fan here," the policeman said.

"It's Mr. Mann's fan, all right," Bugs declared. "It's white, it has four blades, and when you turn it on, it moves from side to side."

Officer Feldman plugged the fan in at the workbench outlet. The whirring fan moved from side to side, spreading a cool breeze.

"Bugs is trying to frame us," Sally said to Officer Feldman.

"Tell that to the Supreme Court," Bugs sneered. "As soon as I learned the fan was gone, I ran here. I saw you two dewdrops hide it behind the plywood. I've suspected all along that the detective agency is just a front for moving hot goods."

Bugs grinned. "After they hid the fan, I followed them back to the accident. They tried to make it look like they had never left."

He rubbed his hands together and gloated. "The poor fools forgot about Bugs Meany, crusader for law and order!"

Sally turned to Encyclopedia with a pleading, do-something look.

"We didn't steal the fan," the detective said to Officer Feldman. "Bugs did."

# What made Encyclopedia so sure?

**(Turn to page 63 for the solution to The Case of the Stolen Fan.)**

# The Case of the Sleeping Dog

**E**lmo was more than Meg Kelly's beagle. He was the only dog in Idaville that could hold three tennis balls in his mouth at once.

Other than that, he had done absolutely nothing special in his whole life. Meg worried over him.

Wednesday morning she came into the Brown Detective Agency all excited.

"I've found a way for Elmo to fulfill himself," she said. "Tomorrow he'll try out for a job as a taster with the Good Eating pet food company."

Pet food companies, she explained, need to find out what dogs like. New meals are tested all the time.

"Every company tries to stay ahead of the other companies," she said. "Pet food is big business."

The job was only for a month. One of the company's

regular taste-testers, a cocker spaniel, was going to Walla Walla for a month's vacation.

"If Elmo gets the job, he'll live the month in luxury and eat like a plow horse," Meg said.

"Can we watch him try out?" Sally asked.

"Sure. The first test begins at Good Eating tomorrow morning at eleven o'clock," Meg said.

The company was only three miles north of Idaville. The detectives arrived there at ten.

Meg greeted them with Elmo in her arms and gloom in her eyes.

"Elmo got hurt half an hour ago," she said. "A box of biscuits slipped off a forklift and hit his paw."

"Oh, no," Sally said. "Will he miss the tryout?"

"No," Meg said. "But even though the injury is small, I have to keep it a secret. The company wants only healthy chowhounds as tasters."

She carried Elmo to a corner for some quiet rest.

The detectives looked around. In a hallway near the testing room was a picnic table. On it were red bowls and yellow bowls filled with dog food.

Beside the bowls was a sheet that read:

### FOR 11 O'Clock TRYOUTS

Below this, the names of the dogs and their owners were listed. The dogs, stalls, and bowls were numbered. Elmo's stall and bowls were number three.

Encyclopedia recognized the names of the other owners: Billy Dean, Frank Barlow, and Hugh Upton. They were sixth-graders.

At eleven sharp the food was brought into the testing room.

In the room were stalls made of panes of glass five feet high.

A red bowl and a yellow bowl were placed in each stall. The bowls held more food than the dogs could finish.

"This is the first of four days of tryouts," a man in a white smock announced. "The better-tasting food is the one the dogs eat more of."

He explained that the panes were there to keep the dogs separated. Otherwise, a free-for-all over the food might break out.

The other job-seekers were a German shepherd, a golden retriever, and a collie. All were purebreds, like Elmo.

"Purebreds make the best tasters," Meg said. "That's because their growth and life span are known."

The dogs were moved to the glass stalls. Elmo always looked bored until mealtime. Now he yelped and whined and pulled at the leash. Chow had arrived.

The leashes were taken off. The dogs raced for the bowls.

Tails wagged. Mouths drooled. Pupils enlarged with pleasure. A few sniffs, and the choice was made.

Each of the four dogs dived into its red bowl.

"Elmo looks like he'll eat everything in sight," Sally said. "Those panes won't stop him."

"That little beagle has some mouth," Hugh marveled.

"You sure you didn't starve him for a week?" Billy asked.

"You ought to get him to a dog doc," Frank said.

But Elmo didn't finish his food. He didn't dash around the panes of his stall, as Sally joked he would, and eat another dog's food.

Rather, he did the opposite.

By and by his jaws slowed. His eyes rolled. Panting faintly, he sank onto his side and went to sleep.

Meg rushed to him. "Something is wrong," she cried. "I'd better get him to the company clinic."

Sally went with her. While she was gone Encyclopedia questioned Hugh, Billy, and Frank.

Each boy claimed he had come to the building a few minutes before the tryout. They said they did not know about Elmo's injury earlier that morning.

By the following day, the animal doctors at the company clinic had made a discovery. Someone had put a fast-acting knockout powder into Elmo's test food.

"Anyone could have done it," Sally said. "Before the test, the bowls of food sat out on a picnic table in plain view."

"It had to be Billy or Frank or Hugh," Meg said. "With Elmo out of the running, their dogs have a better chance of winning the taste-tester's job."

Sally looked at Encyclopedia nervously. "Have you any idea who did it?"

The detective smiled. "Who else but—"

# Who was guilty?

## (Turn to page 64 for the solution to The Case of Sleeping Dog.)

# The Case of the Fig Thieves

**A**gatha Matson, a fourth-grader, lived across the street from the Brown Detective Agency. In her backyard grew the biggest fig tree in Idaville.

Alas, Agatha didn't get to eat many of the figs. Someone else got to them first.

Tuesday morning Encyclopedia and Sally saw Agatha by the big tree. She was talking to Slim Hall and Kirby Phelps. Now and again she shook a finger at them.

"I don't like what I see," Encyclopedia said.

Sally nodded. "Those boys are mean. If a rattlesnake bit them, it would curl up and die."

"I've a hunch Slim and Kirby are the fig thieves," Encyclopedia said. "Agatha must have caught them in the act."

"She's scolding them and they're grinning," Sally said angrily. "They think it's all a big joke."

"This could become ugly," Encyclopedia said. "If Agatha doesn't ease off, Slim and Kirby might rough her up."

"Then let's have action," Sally growled.

She marched out of the detective agency and across the street.

Encyclopedia trailed uneasily. Sally was forever making war on bullies, big or small.

Slim and Kirby were both.

Slim was nearly six feet tall and skinny enough to hide under a racing stripe. His arm muscles looked like fleabites on a noodle. But, oh, how he liked to punch holes in things!

Kirby was barely five feet tall. His size was no short-coming. As a junior-high-school wrestler, he was un-defeated.

"I caught these two stealing figs," Agatha told the detectives. "When my dad comes home, he'll make them wish they had stayed in their own backyard."

"You're barking up the wrong tree," Kirby snarled. "Slim's dog, Blackie, chased a cat, and we chased Blackie. We just stopped under this tree to catch our breath."

"We didn't pick a single fig," Slim said. "Who cares if you don't believe us! You're so far gone you need a search warrant to find your brains."

"Did you actually see them picking figs?" Sally asked Agatha.

"N-No," Agatha admitted. "But I saw them chewing like mad."

"That's good enough," Sally declared.

"Stay out of this," Slim warned Sally. "Go somewhere and unscramble an egg."

"How could we steal her figs?" Kirby demanded. "Use your eyes. We'd need a ladder."

The detectives gazed up at the tree. Kirby was right. The figs on the lowest branch looked too high for anyone to reach.

"Is there a stick they could have used to knock down the figs?" Sally asked.

Agatha shook her head.

Sally looked up at the tree again. She seemed to be thinking over the problem of height. At last she turned to Kirby with a knowing smile.

"You stood on Slim's shoulders," she said.

"You're wacko!" Kirby cried.

"Prove me wrong," Sally challenged. "Stand on Slim's shoulders. Go on!"

"Okay," Kirby said. "We'll do it your way to start. Afterward, I'm going to make you a nurse's pet."

Slim walked to a spot directly under the lowest figs. Kirby got on his shoulders.

"I'll stretch as far as I can," Kirby hollered at the detectives.

He reached above his head. The figs were five to six inches beyond his grasp. He dropped to the ground.

"Now it's my turn," he said, and moved toward Sally.

"Careful," Slim warned. "She likes a fight."

"Don't worry," Kirby replied. "She's only a girl. I can take her."

"Take me where?" Sally scoffed.

Kirby spat and lowered himself into a wrestler's crouch. "I'm going to enjoy this."

His enjoyment ended before it started.

Sally shocked him with an uppercut. She followed with a left hook that knocked him flatter than a pot holder.

Agatha stared at Sally wide-eyed. "He's a star on the wrestling team, and you put him away! I can't believe it."

"Believe me!" Slim howled, and flew at Sally. "Nobody can do that to my pal and get away with it!"

Sally raised her guard. "A girl's got to do what a girl's got to do," she sighed.

A rap on Slim's nose stopped him in his tracks.

A follow-up right to the belly caused his breath to explode with the *whoosh* of a steam engine starting up.

For a time he jiggled about like a boy with shooting pains. Then he flopped upon Kirby, belly to belly.

"Biff, bop, belly flop," Sally quipped.

She smiled down at the two boys at her feet.

Gradually her smile faded.

"Maybe they were telling the truth," she said in a worried voice. "I don't see how they could have reached the figs without a ladder."

"They didn't need a ladder," Encyclopedia replied.

# How had Slim and Kirby reached the figs?

(Turn to page 65 for the solution to The Case of the Fig Thieves.)

# The Case of the Mouse Show

The last Thursday in June the Idaville Youth Club held a mouse show in South Park to help victims of Hurricane Sadie.

The storm had struck Lange City, fifty miles north of Idaville, the week before.

As admission, people brought clothing, or blankets, or bottled water, or food that wouldn't spoil.

Encyclopedia and Sally each dropped packages of hard candy into a box marked SWEETS. Then they headed for the judge's area.

Mr. McRea, the chief judge, was examining a black mouse named Hawthorne.

As its young owner watched nervously, Mr. McRea let Hawthorne run up and down his arm to see how lively he was. He measured the length of Hawthorne's tail. He blew on his fur to see the undercoat.

29

"A mouse must have a long head, but the nose should not be too pointed," Mr. McRea told his audience.

He noted the other features of a winning rodent.

The ears should be big and tulip-shaped and without kinks. The eyes should be bold. The tail should be about as long as the body and smoothly tapered.

"I give Hawthorne eighty-two points," Mr. McRea said.

"A perfect mouse would get one hundred points," Encyclopedia told Sally. "Fifty for color, fifteen for shape, fifteen for condition and carriage, and five each for ears, eyes, snout, and tail."

"Since when are you interested in mice?" Sally said.

"I read up on them before we came here," Encyclopedia admitted.

"I never thought mice could be such a big deal," Sally said.

"This is serious business," Encyclopedia replied. "Show mice are bred like racehorses. To have a chance to win, a mouse must not only be good in all features. It must be of a pure color—black, dove, fawn, chocolate, white, red, or silver."

After watching two more mice being judged, the detectives moved on. They chatted with club members and listened to them share their love of the tiny pets.

At five o'clock the judging ended. The winners were about to be named.

A crowd collected in front of the awards table.

Mr. McRea gave a ten-minute speech on the fun of

raising mice as a hobby. Finally he made the big announcement.

Maisie McArthur won first place. A lovely white house mouse, Maisie slept in a silver punch bowl.

"What does Maisie get for winning?" Sally asked.

"She takes a step toward becoming grand champion of the year," Encyclopedia answered. "That's about all. The prizes haven't changed since Abe Lincoln was President: fifty cents for first place, thirty cents for second, and ten cents for third."

After the second- and third-place winners were named, most of the crowd returned to the mouse pens. The rest started for home.

Encyclopedia bumped into Max Mako. Max was shoving the last of a Venus Peanut Bar into his face.

"I got hungry and ate one of the candy bars I brought for the hurricane relief," Max said sheepishly.

"Seems like you're not alone," Sally said, stooping.

She picked two sourball wrappers off the grass. At that moment Amy Dunn, the Mouse Club secretary, came running up.

"Encyclopedia! Sally!" she cried. "We've got trouble."

She led the detectives to a picnic table at the rear of the show grounds.

Judd Samson, a fifth-grader, stood beside the table, which was loaded with hurricane relief boxes.

"Judd is our club treasurer," Amy said. "Tell Encyclopedia and Sally what happened."

"A little before five o'clock I brought the food boxes in

here," Judd said. "I was getting ready to take a count of what was inside them when I noticed the time. The winning mice were about to be announced. I ran to the awards area. When I got back, the candy—the box marked 'Sweets'—was gone!"

"Is that the only box missing?" Amy asked.

"So far as I can tell," Judd said.

"Was anyone else near the boxes?" Sally asked.

"Stinky Redmond and Casimur Tittleby," Judd answered. "They helped me carry the boxes in here. They left a little before I did to see what mouse won."

"So no one guarded the boxes for several minutes," Sally said.

Judd nodded glumly.

He said, "I was trusted with the job of counting what was in the food boxes. So what happens? Some dirty crook steals forty-three candy bars while I'm off finding out what mouse won."

Sally asked where Stinky Redmond was.

Judd shrugged. "I haven't seen him since he took off for the awards."

"Why did Stinky help with the boxes?" Amy said. "When has he ever helped anyone but himself?"

"Never," Sally agreed. "I wish we could prove he's guilty!"

"We don't have to," Encyclopedia replied.

# What did Encyclopedia mean?

(Turn to page 66 for the solution to The Case of the Mouse Show.)

# The Case of the Tied-up Twins

Encyclopedia and Sally were biking through South Park when they came upon an odd sight. Two blond men were bound together by a long rope tied around their waists.

Watching them closely was a big woman wearing a blue jacket.

"Ten minutes to go!" she called.

The blond men let out a tired whoop and raised their thumbs to each other.

Nearby stood a group of photographers, TV camera operators, reporters, and curious onlookers. Encyclopedia spotted Pablo Pizzaro, Idaville's greatest boy artist.

"What's this all about?" the detective asked.

"It's a performance art contest," said Pablo.

"You mean performing arts," Sally corrected him.

"No, performance art," Pablo replied. "In performing

arts, people do usual things like dance or sing or play the piano. Performance art is different. People try to create art with their lives."

"Being tied together is art?" inquired Encyclopedia.

Pablo gave a deep and dreamy sigh. "The performance artist tries to show life's struggle in a new way. It's meaningful. It's now."

"It's horsefeathers," Sally said.

"I see you do not understand," Pablo declared.

"I understand, all right," Sally said. "Art today is anything you can get away with."

"You have to look at living art with an open mind," Pablo insisted.

"I'd rather look at meat loaf," Sally said.

The remark stung Pablo. He reacted like a rabbit. The tip of his nose quivered.

When his nose calmed down, he explained the contest that kept two men roped together.

It was staged by the A-1 Natural Rope Company. The purpose was to prove that A-1's natural rope was the longest-lasting in America. "No Nylon, No Rayon, No Dacron—All Natural!" was the company's motto.

"Two persons have to stay tied together with the same piece of A-1 Natural Rope seventeen feet in length," Pablo said. "They can only take the rope off for an hour a day in private."

"The rope company is over in Glenn City," Sally said. "Why is the contest in Idaville?"

"The company wanted the last week of the contest to

take place here," Pablo said. "It's great publicity. Idaville is famous. Besides, we have beaches."

Encyclopedia pointed at the brothers and asked, "Do those two ever go into the ocean?"

"Every morning," Pablo answered. "The rope doesn't bother them. They time their movements perfectly."

"Where are the others in the contest?" Sally asked.

"At the start there were twenty pairs," Pablo said. "Nineteen dropped out in a hurry."

He told the detectives why. One of the rules was that the pair had to stay tied together for almost all of the 31,536,000 seconds that the contest would last.

"When the others realized that many seconds were not just a few days but a year, they quit," Pablo said. "Only the Hanson brothers over there stuck it out."

"With the contest down to one pair, the rope company must be really disappointed," Sally said.

"And how," replied Pablo. "So to add news interest, kids were allowed to compete today, the last day. They don't have to be roped. But every half hour they have to do a piece of performance art for three minutes."

He pointed to his left.

Encyclopedia saw a man in a blue jacket. In front of him were Stinky Redmond, Tessie Bottoms, and Alice Cohen.

"The man and the big woman are judges," Pablo said. "He's making sure each kid does something artistic."

Stinky walked around like a boy who had just stepped in something mushy.

Tessie pushed a stick into the ground and jumped straight up in the air.

Alice lay on her back without moving.

"Good grief, it's crazy crackers time!" Sally exclaimed.

"It's performance art," Pablo corrected. "Stinky is acting like a turkey caught in the rain. Tessie is doing standing pole vaults. Alice is taking on the personality of someone else."

"Who lies without moving?" Encyclopedia asked.

"Bugs Meany after a fight with Sally," Pablo said.

Encyclopedia chuckled, then grew thoughtful. "Did a judge watch the brothers all the time?"

"Most of the time, yes," Pablo answered. "But not all the time. The contest is run on the honor code."

Suddenly the big woman blew a whistle.

"The year is up!" she cried. "You've won!"

The brothers jumped and shouted. They congratulated themselves as if they'd done the nation a great service.

"Art triumphs over every hardship!" Pablo sang. "The brothers will be hired by A-1 to do TV commercials. They'll get rich."

"How about the kids?" Sally asked.

"The winning kid gets a bicycle," Pablo replied.

"I don't know who will win the bicycle," Encyclopedia murmured. "But the brothers won't make a penny."

# Why was Encyclopedia so certain?

**(Turn to page 67 for the solution to The Case of the Tied-up Twins.)**

39

# The Case of Wilford's Big Deal

**V**era Pincus rushed into the Brown Detective Agency.

"Take a last look at the old me," she cried.

"Old? Golly, you're only nine," Sally said.

"I don't mean age," Vera said. "I mean poor. The new me is going to be so rich I can buy Rhode Island and ship it to Florida for the winter."

"Who told you that?" Encyclopedia asked.

"Wilford Wiggins," Vera replied.

Encyclopedia groaned. He always groaned at the mention of Wilford Wiggins.

Wilford was a high-school dropout and as hardworking as a jellyfish. He lay around all morning dreaming of ways to cheat little kids out of their savings.

Wilford's phony deals never succeeded, however. Encyclopedia was always there to nip them into duds.

"What's Wilford selling now?" Sally asked. "The world's fastest stopwatch?"

"Wilford told me he's given up cheating," Vera said. "He's gone straight."

As straight, Encyclopedia thought, as a crowbar.

"Wilford called a secret meeting for five o'clock today at the city dump," Vera said.

"If he offers you a fast deal, see a lawyer," Sally said. "And if the lawyer says it's okay, see another lawyer."

Vera laughed but looked uncertain.

She laid twenty-five cents on the gas can beside Encyclopedia. "I'll hire you to make sure Wilford has really turned honest."

"We'll take the case," Sally said eagerly.

Wilford was starting his sales pitch when the detectives and Vera arrived at the city dump.

"Come closer, come closer," Wilford chanted at the crowd of small children. "I don't want any of my little pals to miss this chance of a lifetime."

"Aw, get on with it," a boy shouted. "Let's hear some big-bucks talk."

"Stick with me and you'll see nothing but big bucks, friend," Wilford yawped. "Take a look!"

He pointed to the sky.

"I don't see anything," the boy said.

"When night comes," Wilford proclaimed, "you'll see the answer to your dreams. Every star is worth fifty bucks!"

He paused to let his words sink in.

"Stars have numbers, but few have names," he resumed. "So I'm forming a company, Name Your Star. It will offer people a chance to name a star after anyone or anything. The price will be fifty dollars a name."

"Nobody here has fifty dollars," Vera protested.

"I'm not selling stars to my pals," Wilford said. "I'm giving you a chance to buy shares in my Name Your Star company at a special low, low price!"

"How can you be sure that the star a customer chooses hasn't already got a name?" a girl asked.

"A chart of all the unnamed stars you can see has been made by my partner, Professor Hans Zingler, the great German astronomer," Wilford said. "Unfortunately, he met with an accident this morning."

Professor Zingler's plane from Germany had landed that morning at eight o'clock, Wilford said. The plane came in from the south. It nosed up to a gate at the north end of the airport, where international flights unloaded.

There something went wrong, Wilford said. The covered bridge that passengers walk through from the plane to the airport building didn't work. The passengers had to leave by a set of stairs rolled to the door.

"As Professor Zingler stepped onto the top stair," Wilford went on, "the bright sun hit him directly in the eyes, half blinding him. He dropped his suitcase. It broke open. The wind scattered what was inside—the charts of unnamed stars."

"Where does that leave us?" a girl demanded.

"Professor Zingler has sent to Germany for copies of the charts," Wilford said. "They'll be here in a few days."

"Then we'd better wait," a boy said.

"I can't wait," Wilford declared. "I need to start the company before somebody beats me to it. I'll have to raise the cash in New York City or Chicago."

Wilford fell silent for a long moment. He seemed to be wrestling with the problem.

"I'll never forgive myself if I let my little pals miss out on such easy money," he said mournfully. "So I'll tell you what I'm going to do."

He leaned forward and flashed an oily smile.

"I'll let you buy shares in my company for five dollars a share if you buy now. Today only, I'll throw in the big one—you can name a star for free! Tomorrow it'll cost fifty bucks."

Excitement swept the crowd. There were enough stars to sell to all the people in the world at fifty bucks apiece.

By owning a little of the company, every kid in the dump would be worth millions!

It was too good a deal to miss.

The children lined up to buy shares.

"Encyclopedia, don't let Wilford walk off with their savings!" Sally pleaded.

"He won't get a cent," Encyclopedia said.

# What was Wilford's slip?

(Turn to page 68 for the solution to The Case of Wilford's Big Deal.)

# The Case of the Fake Soup Can

**C**hester Jenkins, one of Encyclopedia's pals, was known to eat so fast that his knife and fork gave off sparks.

The size of his waistline caused a few unfriendly kids to call him a walking tomato.

"Chester starts a seven-day diet tomorrow," Encyclopedia said.

"I hope he doesn't finish it in one day," replied Sally.

The detectives were biking to Chester's house. He had invited them to a professional soccer game in nearby Glenn City.

Chester was standing on his front lawn when the detectives arrived. He was jawing with Ed Burgess.

Stomach for stomach, the two boys were an even match.

"Ed's folks don't like to take him to a restaurant," Sally

said. "The last time they did, he looked at the menu and ordered page three."

The two champion eaters were going at each other hot and heavy.

"Milk of human kindness," Ed barked.

"Cheese it," Chester responded.

"Full of beans."

"Cool as a cucumber."

Roscoe Tenn, one of Bugs Meany's Tigers, came by. He stopped to listen.

"What's this all about?" he inquired.

"Beats me," Sally said.

"Is anything in your room in apple-pie order?" Ed flung at Chester.

"Full of ginger," Chester flung back.

"Duel with me and you'll end up in the soup," Ed warned.

"Tight as a clam."

"Ham actor."

"Can't these two blimps talk about anything but eats?" Roscoe muttered in disgust. "I'm going home."

He hoofed it for the shortcut behind Chester's house.

"We're having a food-sayings duel," Chester told the detectives, and swung back into action. "Other fish to fry."

"She's a peach," Ed retorted.

"Takes the cake."

"Brown as a berry." Ed spoke bravely, but he was clearly struggling to keep up.

"Don't flounder," Chester snapped.

Ed sneered. "Full of beans."

"A repeat!" Chester cried triumphantly, and blasted away. "Good egg! Red herring! Couch potato! Top banana! Cut the mustard! Pie in the sky!"

Ed threw up his hands. "Okay, I'm licked."

"That's the way cookie crumbles," Chester said.

"Nuts," Ed grumbled, and trudged off in defeat.

"You were great, Chester," Sally said.

"Thanks," Chester said. "We'd better be on our way. The soccer game starts in an hour."

The detectives followed him up to his room to get the tickets. Chester took a can labeled NEW ENGLAND CLAM CHOWDER from a shelf above his desk.

"This isn't a can you buy at a supermarket," he said. "It's a tiny safe."

He unscrewed the bottom of the can and peered inside.

"Empty!" he gasped. "Somebody stole the tickets!"

"Who knew you had tickets?" Sally asked.

"Lots of kids," Chester said. "I've talked about the game for days."

"But who knew you kept them in that can?" Sally said.

Chester frowned. "Ed Burgess knew. I showed it to him before we went outside."

"What was Ed doing here?" Sally asked.

"His aunt bought him a French cookbook. He wanted me to try out a fancy cheesecake recipe this afternoon," Chester replied.

"Ed brings over a cookbook," Encyclopedia said, "even though he knows you won't have time to bake a cheesecake before the soccer game. How interesting . . ."

Sally said, "First Ed gets Chester to talk about the game. Then he gets him to tell where he keeps the tickets."

Chester winced. "That's just what happened. I guess I wanted to show off the can. I never dreamed he'd steal from me."

Sally looked puzzled. "How could Ed have stolen the tickets without Chester seeing him?"

"Yes, how?" Chester said. "After I showed him the fake can of New England Clam Chowder, we left the room. Ed never touched the can."

"Who suggested the food-sayings duel, you or Ed?" Encyclopedia asked.

"Ed," Chester answered.

"So," Encyclopedia said. "Ed had a partner."

"What?" Sally asked, at a loss. "Who?"

"Roscoe Tenn," Encyclopedia answered. "When Roscoe said he was going home, he really went up to your room by the back door and stole the tickets."

"No one would have seen him," Chester said thoughtfully. "My folks are at work. So is my sister. The house is empty. But how did Roscoe know where the tickets were hidden?"

Encyclopedia smiled. "Ed told him."

"Ed never spoke a word to Roscoe!" Sally objected.

"Oh, yes, he did," corrected Encyclopedia.

# How did Ed tell Roscoe the hiding place?

(Turn to page 69 for the solution to The Case of the Fake Soup Can.)

# The Case of the Shoeshine War

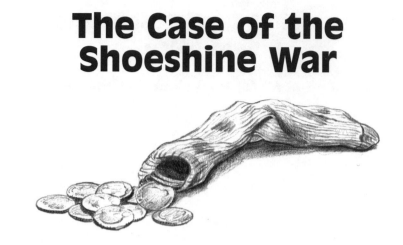

Chester Jenkins's twin sister, Candice, ate nearly as much as he did.

Around the neighborhood she was known by many names, including the Walking Fork.

Candice took the kidding with a sense of humor and went on eating.

To keep herself in goodies, she had gone into business. She shined shoes on the corner of Fifth and Main Streets.

Saturday morning Encyclopedia and Sally stopped at the corner. Candice wasn't in sight.

On the sidewalk were the tools of her trade: a folding chair, a metal footrest fixed to a box that held cleaners, polishes, brushes, and ten-ounce cloths called rags.

Halfway down the block the door of Ted's Donut Shop opened. Candice stepped forth eating a donut.

"You shouldn't leave your things out like this," Sally told her. "Someone might take them."

"I lost my head," Candice replied. "Today is Ted's Donut Shop's grand opening. You get two donuts for the price of one all day. . . ."

She stared at the box by the chair.

"The sock with my money!" she yelped. "It's gone!"

"Oh, dear," Sally said. "How much was in it?"

"I always start work with ten dollars to make change," Candice replied. "Today I was going to try something different. I brought only quarters."

"If a customer gives you a five-dollar bill, he won't like getting all his change in coins," Sally observed. "That's extra weight to carry around."

"Exactly the point," Candice said. "To get rid of some of the weight, he'll tip more."

"What a great bit of thinking!" Sally exclaimed.

Encyclopedia said, "The thief had to move fast while you were in the donut shop. That means he knew where to look. Who knows about the sock?"

"Two of Bugs Meany's Tigers," Candice answered. "Mugsy Moonsooner and Jimbo Dawson. We're in the same business."

Encyclopedia glanced up the street. Mugsy and Jimbo were on the next two corners, waiting for customers.

"They've declared a rag-popping war," Candice said. "Lucky for me they brag better than they shine."

"Then let's have action," Sally said.

They began with Mugsy.

"We'd like to talk with you," Encyclopedia said quietly.

"Interview me?" Mugsy said. "Listen, I'm so big I turn down a hundred interviews a year. However, as a special favor, I'll talk to you. I'm the Idaville rag-popping champion. Watch this."

He picked up a cloth and pretended to shine his shoe on the metal footrest. Between rapid back-and-forth strokes he brought the ends of the cloth together and snapped them wide, *pop pop chuckha chuckha pop pop.*

"Oh, I do make such sweet music!" he sang.

"Sounds like a school bus clumping along on three cylinders," Sally murmured.

"Candice says someone stole her sock with ten dollars in it a few minutes ago," said Encyclopedia.

"The only thing I've stolen from Ms. Fatso is some of her customers," Mugsy bragged.

"Liar!" Candice shot back. "You use rags I wouldn't hit a cockroach with."

"Where were you when Candice left her corner for the donut shop?" Sally asked.

"I mind my own business," Mugsy growled. He folded his arms tightly across his chest. "End of interview."

"I think he's the one," Sally said as they walked over to Jimbo.

Encyclopedia gave Jimbo his friendliest smile. "How's business this morning?"

"Slow so far, but it's early," Jimbo replied. "It'll pick up. There's no shine like a Jimbo shine."

"We'd like to ask you a few questions," Sally said.

"Go ahead," Jimbo said. "Although I'm famous, I still talk to my fans. I still walk the street and sign autographs. How many famous people will do that?"

"Candice keeps money for making change in a sock in her shoeshine box," Sally told him.

"It was stolen," Candice piped up.

Jimbo snorted. "This kid's belly weighs more than her brain if she thinks I robbed her. What do I need quarters for when I have a million dollars' worth of talent? I'm the best rag-popper anywhere. Now be kind to yourself and get lost!"

The detectives and Candice walked away. When they reached Candice's shoeshine stand, Encyclopedia halted and closed his eyes in thought.

"Maybe someone else stole my money," Candice suggested.

"I doubt it," Sally said. "Mugsy and Jimbo want to run you off Main Street. They're after all the business."

Candice nodded. "Both had time to steal my money and hide it before you questioned them. But which one? Jimbo or Mugsy?"

"Give Encyclopedia a minute and we'll find out," Sally said confidently.

Encyclopedia opened his eyes. "The one who stole your money, Candice, is—"

# Who stole Candice's money?

(Turn to page 70 for the solution to The Case of the Shoeshine War.)

# Solutions

# The Case of the
# Shower Singers

The singers were Dale Manning, Walter Blake, Stan Z. Zamora, Oscar March, Maria Woods, and Oliver Grossman.

Once he had the key to the code—Mrs. Galan's interest in names—Encyclopedia easily cracked it.

The words—*aria alter liver scar ale tan*—were the singers' first names with the first letter of each name left off.

When the first letters were put back, the words became names: *Dale, Walter, Stan, Oscar, Maria,* and *Oliver.*

Encyclopedia then took the first letters and put them in the same order as the words of the code.

Thus, the winner was *m w o o d s,* or Maria Woods.

# The Case of the Invisible Writing

Bugs Meany dreamed up the story about making writing disappear.

He wanted to trade for Kitty's key lime pie.

Once he got her to write her name with a red pencil, he thought the pie was his.

But he overlooked Encyclopedia's fast brain.

Using an ordinary flashlight like Bugs's, you too can make red writing disappear. All you need is a red bulb to shine on the red letters in the dark.

As Encyclopedia knew, you can't see red letters when a red light is shining on them.

Kitty's grandmother got her pie.

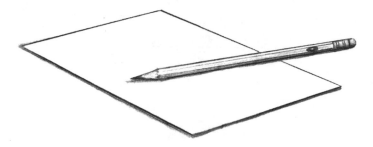

# The Case of the Stolen Fan

By his own account, Bugs never saw the electric desk fan when it wasn't turning.

Mr. Mann, Bugs said, had raced from his office to the accident. That meant Mr. Mann left the fan still turning.

Yet Bugs said he knew the fan in the garage belonged to Mr. Mann because, among other features, it had four blades.

Only if the fan was stopped could Bugs have seen the blades, Encyclopedia realized.

To steal the fan, Bugs first had to unplug it. When the blades stopped, he saw how many there were—not two, not three, but four!

Bugs's attempt to frame the detectives stopped, too.

# The Case of the Sleeping Dog

Hugh, Billy, and Frank all claimed to have come to the pet food building just a few minutes before the tryout.

Frank lied. He had to have come earlier because he knew Elmo had been hurt.

He also knew where to put the sleeping powder. The sheet on the picnic table told him the number (three) of Elmo's stall and bowls.

During the test, Sally said, "Those panes won't stop him." By *panes* she meant the glass panes of Elmo's stall.

Knowing Elmo had been hurt, Frank thought she said *pains*.

He gave himself away by suggesting, "You ought to get him to a dog doc."

# The Case of the Fig Thieves

Kirby showed Sally he couldn't reach the figs by standing on Slim's shoulders.

That's when Encyclopedia figured out how the boys had reached the figs without a ladder.

They had simply swapped positions.

Instead of Kirby standing on Slim's shoulders, Slim stood on Kirby's shoulders.

Slim's longer arms allowed him to reach the fruit without any trouble.

Kirby and Slim admitted stealing figs all summer. They promised to stop.

Sally made sure they did.

# The Case of the Mouse Show

Encyclopedia didn't have to prove who was guilty. Judd did it for him.

Judd said he was getting ready to count the food in the boxes when he rushed to see what mouse won.

Later, forgetting what he had said, he told Encyclopedia and Sally, "Some dirty crook steals forty-three candy bars while I'm off finding out what mouse won."

He could not have known how many candy bars were stolen if he hadn't yet counted them.

Unless, of course, he had stolen them himself.

Judd returned the candy.

# The Case of the Tied-up Twins

A rule of the contest was that the *same* seventeen-foot rope had be to used throughout the year.

After the contest, Encyclopedia quietly measured the brothers' rope. It was seventeen feet.

It should have been shorter.

A seventeen-foot rope of natural fiber will shrink up to a foot if left in water a few hours. The brothers had gone into the ocean "every morning" for a week.

To make sure their rope didn't break with wear and put them out of the contest, the brothers had changed ropes many times. They were disqualified for cheating.

The lone winner was Alice Cohen. She won the bicycle.

# The Case of Wilford's Big Deal

Wilford had no way of getting charts of the unnamed stars. So he made up Professor Zingler and a fancy story.

He said the early morning sun hit Professor Zingler directly in the eyes as he stepped from the plane. Half blinded, the professor dropped his suitcase with the charts.

Impossible!

The morning sun is in the east. The plane was pointed north, having nosed up to the north end of the airport.

To face the morning sun, the passengers would have had to leave by the plane's east side—that is, the right side.

Passengers normally leave an airplane by the left side, occasionally by the rear, but never by the right side.

The kids of Idaville got to keep their savings.

# The Case of the Fake Soup Can

Ed and Roscoe had a plan.

Ed was to find out where Chester had hidden the tickets. Then he would pass the hiding place along to Roscoe during the food-sayings duel.

Ed slipped a clue into two food sayings. He pointed Roscoe to the clues by putting them in extra-long sayings.

The sayings were: "Is anything *in your room* ever in apple-pie order?" and "Duel with me, and you'll end up *in the soup*."

Roscoe caught on immediately. He sneaked into Chester's room and lifted the tickets from the fake soup can.

Ed returned the tickets.

# The Case of the Shoeshine War

Jimbo was the thief.

When questioned about the missing money, he couldn't help bragging.

"What do I need quarters for when I have a million dollars' worth of talent?" he said.

That was his mistake!

He was told only that "Candice keeps money for making change in a sock in her shoeshine box."

Yet he knew what only the thief could know.

The missing money was in quarters.

Jimbo returned the quarters to Candice.

Then he quit shining shoes on Main Street.

# About the Author

Donald J. Sobol is the award-winning author of more than sixty-five books for young readers. He lives in Florida with his wife, Rose, who is also an author. They have three grown children. The Encyclopedia Brown books have been translated into fourteen languages.

# About the Illustrator

Warren Chang is a graduate of the Art Center College of Design in California. He was born in Monterey, California, and currently lives in Brooklyn, New York, where he specializes in illustrating book covers and interiors. In addition, he teaches illustration at Pratt Institute in New York City.